Tales from Deckawoo Drive

3 Books in 1

3 Adventures on Deckawoo Drive

D0036505

Kate DiCamillo
illustrated by Chris Van Dusen

CANDLEWICK PRESS

Books for early readers
FROM KATE DICAMILLO AND CHRIS VAN DUSEN

A Piglet Named Mercy

Mercy Watson
Mercy Watson to the Rescue
Mercy Watson Goes for a Ride
Mercy Watson Fights Crime
Mercy Watson: Princess in Disguise
Mercy Watson Thinks Like a Pig
Mercy Watson: Something Wonky This Way Comes

Tales from Deckawoo Drive
Leroy Ninker Saddles Up
Francine Poulet Meets the Ghost Raccoon
Where Are You Going, Baby Lincoln?
Eugenia Lincoln and the Unexpected Package

Tales from Deckawoo Drive

Contents

VOLUME ONE

Leroy Ninker Saddles Up

1

VOLUME TWO

Francine Poulet Meets the Ghost Raccoon

95

VOLUME THREE

Where Are You Going, Baby Lincoln?

195

To Amy and her class of heroes
K. D. and C. V.

Tales from Deckawoo Drive

Volume One

Leroy Ninker Saddles Up

Chapter One

Leroy Ninker worked at the Bijou Drive-In Theater concession stand.

It was Leroy's job to pour drinks and butter popcorn and smile a very large smile.

At the concession stand, Leroy Ninker said, "Thank you very much!"

He said, "Extra butter on that?"

He also said, "Yippie-i-oh."

Leroy Ninker said "Yippie-i-oh" because Leroy Ninker had a dream. He wanted to be a cowboy.

On Wednesday nights, the Bijou Drive-In Theater ran a Western double feature, and Leroy Ninker stood and watched in wonder as the great white expanse of the Bijou screen filled with purple mountains, wide-open plains, and cowboys.

The cowboys wore ten-gallon hats. They wore boots. They carried lassos. The cowboys were men who cast long shadows and knew how to fight injustice. They were men who were never, ever afraid.

"Yippie-i-oh," Leroy Ninker whispered to the screen. "That is the life for me. A cowboy is who I was meant to be."

"Who are you whispering to?" said Beatrice Leapaleoni.

Beatrice was the ticket seller at the Bijou. Once all the tickets were sold and the movie had begun, Beatrice joined Leroy Ninker in the concession stand so that she could eat popcorn and watch the movie.

"I am not whispering," said Leroy Ninker very loudly. "Cowboys do not whisper."

"Can I make a point?" said Beatrice Leapaleoni. "Can I make a simple observation?"

"Yes," said Leroy.

"All these cowboys," said Beatrice, "what have they got?"

"Hats," said Leroy Ninker as he stared at the screen. "And also boots."

6

"Yep," said Beatrice. "What else?"

"Lassos," said Leroy. He put his hand on his lasso.

"And?" said Beatrice.

"Tracking abilities?" said Leroy.

Beatrice heaved a heavy sigh. "I am thinking of something that you can actually see. Something right in front of you." She paused. "Something that the cowboys are sitting on."

Leroy Ninker took off his hat and scratched his head.

Beatrice sighed again. "Horses, Leroy," she said. "Every cowboy needs a horse."

Leroy Ninker was a small man with a big dream. He was also the kind of man who knew the truth when he heard it. Suddenly, his hat and his lasso and his boots and his *yippie-i-oh*s didn't feel like enough. Beatrice Leapaleoni was right. How could he ever hope to be a cowboy, a real cowboy, a true cowboy, without a horse?

"Yep," said Beatrice, "you've got a problem. You've got to procure a horse. But don't worry, I happen to have the solution for you right here." She held up a copy of the *Gizzford Gazette*. "Listen," she said. Beatrice adjusted her glasses. She cleared her throat.

"'Horse for sale,'" Beatrice Leapaleoni read. "'Old but good. Very exceptionally cheap.'"

"Yippie-i-oh," said Leroy Ninker. He took out his wallet and counted his money. He looked at Beatrice Leapaleoni. He said, "How much is very exceptionally cheap?"

"I guess you won't know until you ask," said Beatrice.

"Right," said Leroy. He counted his money again. "I hope I have enough."

"Listen," said Beatrice. "What you have to do here is take fate in your hands and wrestle it to the ground."

"Right!" said Leroy. "I am going to wrestle fate. I am going to get a horse!"

"There you go," said Beatrice. She tore the ad out of the paper and handed it to Leroy.

"Yippie-i-oh," said Leroy. He carefully folded the piece of paper and put it in his wallet.

"Don't forget to inspect the teeth," said Beatrice Leapaleoni. "And the hooves. That is what matters with horses. Teeth. And hooves."

"Teeth and hooves," said Leroy Ninker.

"Exactly," said Beatrice.

★ ★ ★

10

That night, Leroy Ninker did not sleep well. He dreamed of horses. Specifically, he dreamed of teeth and hooves.

Also, he dreamed of Beatrice Leapaleoni. In his dream, she kept clearing her throat and saying, "Take fate in your hands, take fate in your hands, take fate in your hands."

"And then what?" said Leroy Ninker in the dream.

"And then," said Beatrice Leapaleoni in a very solemn voice, "you must wrestle it to the ground."

Chapter Two

The next morning after breakfast, Leroy Ninker put his hat on his head and his boots on his feet. He consulted the ad from the *Gizzford Gazette*. He read aloud the address of the horse for sale.

"'Route sixteen, third house on the left,'" said Leroy Ninker. And then he said it again, "Route sixteen, third house on the left," just to make sure he had it right.

Leroy folded the ad back up. He put it in his wallet. He adjusted his hat. He was now prepared to take fate in his hands and wrestle it to the ground. He was ready to procure a horse. Leroy set out walking.

The sun was high above his head, and the sky was very blue. As Leroy walked, he imagined that he was on the open plain.

A car drove by. "Look, Mama!" A boy in the backseat of the car pointed at Leroy. "It's a very tiny cowboy."

Leroy stood up straighter.

"I am a cowboy on his way to procure a horse," he said. "I am a man wrestling fate to the ground."

Another car drove by. Someone threw a can out the window. The can hit Leroy Ninker in the head.

"Dang nib it," said Leroy. He stopped
and took off his hat. He rubbed at his
head. "Don't get agitated," he told himself.
"Just keep thinking about your horse."

Leroy Ninker put his hat back on his
head and started walking again. He thought
about his horse. *I hope he is a fast horse,* he
thought. *And I hope that he is strong. I will call
him Tornado.*

Leroy found this name so pleasing that he had to stop walking and hold himself very still and properly consider the glory of the word.

"Tornado," Leroy whispered.

And then he shouted it: *"Tornado!"*

It was the most perfect name for a horse ever.

"Tornado!" shouted Leroy Ninker again. "Yippie-i-oh."

The cowboy started to run. He was heading to meet the horse of his dreams! There was no time to waste!

"I'm on my way, Tornado!" shouted Leroy Ninker as he ran down the side of the road.

By the time Leroy made it to his destination, it was late afternoon and his feet hurt.

"What can I do for you?" said the woman who answered the door.

"I am here about the horse," said Leroy.

"You're interested in Maybelline?" said the woman.

"Maybelline?" said Leroy.

"Follow me, Hank," said the woman.

"Hank?" said Leroy.

The woman walked to the back of the house. Leroy followed her. "Since you are asking," said the woman over her shoulder, "my name is Patty LeMarque. Maybelline is right over here."

Patty LeMarque climbed a fence.

Leroy climbed the fence, too.

"There she is," said Patty LeMarque. She waved her arm in the direction of a horse standing in a field. "There is Maybelline."

At the sound of her name, the horse turned and came trotting toward them. She whinnied. She was a big horse, and her whinny was very loud.

"Maybelline," said Patty LeMarque, "meet Hank."

The horse whinnied again. She opened her mouth wide. Leroy took advantage of her mouth being open to look at her teeth. There weren't a lot of them. As far as he could tell, there were four in total.

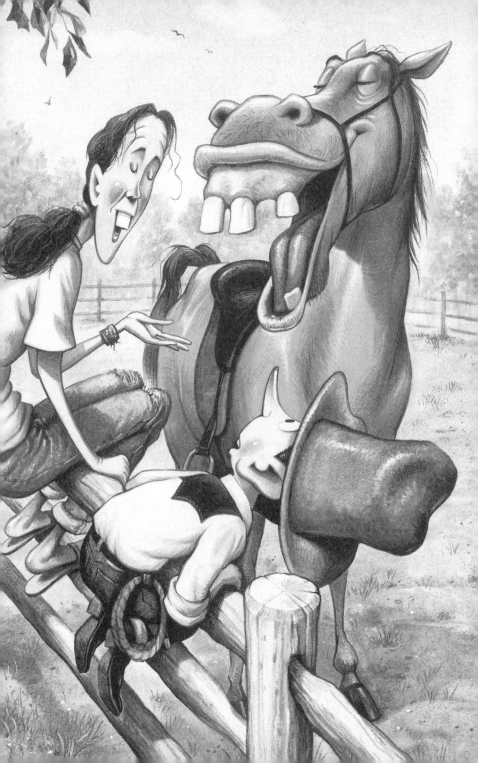

How many teeth was a horse supposed to have? Beatrice Leapaleoni had not said.

Leroy Ninker looked down at the horse's hooves. There were four of them, too.

That seemed good.

"Yippie-i-oh," said Leroy Ninker.

The horse put her nose right up in his face. It was a large nose. There were whiskers on it, and it smelled very much like the nose of a horse.

"She likes you," said Patty LeMarque. "Ain't that something? Maybelline don't like everybody. In fact, there's a whole raft of people she don't like. She is a particular horse, if you don't mind me saying so."

"I don't mind you saying so," said Leroy.

He put out his hand and touched the horse's nose. It was damp and velvety. Leroy felt his heart tumble and roll inside of him. Oh, to be a cowboy with a horse! To ride into the sunset! To ride into the wind! To be brave and true and cast a large, horsey shadow!

"Maybelline," said Leroy Ninker.

"That's her name," said Patty LeMarque.

"I'll take her," said Leroy.

Chapter Three

"Now, Maybelline's old," said Patty LeMarque, "and I am moving, and where I am moving to, they don't take horses. My main goal here is to make sure that Maybelline goes to a home where she is loved up good through all her older, more golden years. You understand what I'm saying, Hank?"

"Yippie-i-oh," said Leroy.

"I ain't looking for money is what I am saying. I am looking for love for Maybelline. And I am just going on my instinctuals here, but my instinctuals tell me that you are the right little fellow for this horse. So now I am going to tell you some things about Maybelline. Listen up, Hank."

"Yippie-i-oh," said Leroy.

Patty LeMarque looked at him. She squinted. "I don't know what that means, Hank," she said.

"Okay," said Leroy. "It means okay."

"If okay is what you mean, Hank," said Patty LeMarque, "then just flat out say it. Be a straightforward communicator, like me."

"Okay," said Leroy.

"Okay!" said Patty LeMarque. "Here are the things about Maybelline. There are three items you got to remember. Item one is that she is the kind of horse who enjoys the heck out of a compliment. You got to talk sweet to Maybelline, understand?"

"Yippie-i-oh," said Leroy.

"Itchie-pitchie-poo, Hank," said Patty LeMarque. "Say what you mean and mean what you say."

"Okay," said Leroy.

"There you go!" said Patty LeMarque. "Item two about Maybelline is that she is a horse who eats a lot of grub. And when I say a lot of grub, I mean something real specified. What I mean is this horse eats A. Lot. Of. Grub."

"Okay," said Leroy. He nodded. "A lot of grub."

"Item three is that Maybelline is the kind of horse who gets lonesome quick. What I mean by that is that she is not the kind of horse who cares to be left behind. This is the most important item, Hank. Do not leave Maybelline alone for long, or you will live to rue and regret the day."

"Rue and regret the day," said Leroy. "Okay."

"All right, then," said Patty LeMarque. "She's all saddled up and ready to go. Let me give you a hand here, Hank, since you are kind of a short little gentleman who looks to be in need of assistance with some of life's more overwhelming necessities."

Patty LeMarque helped Leroy Ninker up on Maybelline's back, and right away Leroy Ninker noticed that the world was different from the top of a horse. The colors were deeper. The sun shone brighter. The birds sang more sweetly.

Also, Patty LeMarque seemed shorter and a tiny bit less bossy.

"Giddy-up," said Leroy Ninker to his horse.

Nothing happened.

Leroy Ninker slapped the reins. "Giddy-up," he said again.

Maybelline stood without moving.

"Hank," said Patty LeMarque, "I don't believe that you were listening to me even one tiny bit when I listed out them three items. You got to listen in this world, Hank. You got to pay attention to the informational bits that people share with you."

"Okay," said Leroy.

"Okay, then. Listen up. If I were you, I would cogitate on item one right about now."

"Do what?" said Leroy.

"Compliment her," whispered Patty LeMarque. "Give the horse some pretty words."

Leroy Ninker looked down at Maybelline's bony back. He counted the knobs in her spine. He tried to think of some pretty words. Did he even know any pretty words?

Leroy thought very hard.

And finally, Leroy spoke. He opened his mouth and said the sweetest words he could think of. He said, "You are the most beautified horse in the whole wide green world."

The horse pricked up her ears. She twitched the left ear to the right and the right ear to the left. Both ears quivered hopefully.

Emboldened, Leroy Ninker leaned forward and spoke directly into the right ear. He said, "You are the sweetest blossom in springtime."

Maybelline picked up her right front hoof. She held it high in the air.

"Good job, Hank," said Patty LeMarque.

"You are a pure flower of horsiness!" said Leroy Ninker.

Maybelline began to walk.

"Well, look at you, Hank," said Patty LeMarque. "It seems you got a talent for poeticals."

"Oh, Maybelline!" shouted Leroy. "You are the brightest star in the velvety nighttime sky!"

Maybelline broke into a trot.

"Good-bye, Maybelline!" shouted Patty LeMarque. "Good luck, Hank. Remember them other two items! And listen to the people of the world when they offer you informational bits!"

Patty LeMarque held up a hand and waved, and Leroy waved back and then Patty LeMarque disappeared.

Maybelline (Leroy's horse!) was going very, very fast.

Chapter Four

Leroy Ninker held on tight. He thought of more pretty words, and he said them.

"Sweetness," said the cowboy. "Lovely one. Beloved."

The horse went faster.

"Maybelline of my dreams!" shouted Leroy Ninker.

The world was a green and gold blur, and Leroy was happier than he had ever been in his life. Maybelline ran and ran and ran.

The horse ran until the sun was low in the sky and the shadows were long and sad.

"Maybelline," said Leroy into Maybelline's left ear, "it is time for the two of us to head home."

Maybelline nickered. She slowed down to a trot. And then she stopped entirely. Leroy Ninker slid forward in the saddle.

"Giddy-up, my beautiful one," said Leroy.

But Maybelline held still.

"Yippie-i-oh, my beloved," said Leroy. "We are homeward bound."

Maybelline looked to the left, and then she looked to the right. She let out a long whinny.

"Oh," said Leroy. "I get it." He slid off Maybelline's back. He took hold of the reins. "Come on, horse of my heart," he said. "I will show you the way home."

Leroy walked ahead, and Maybelline followed behind, and every once in a while, she would give Leroy a friendly little bump with her nose, pushing him forward. And in this way, the cowboy and his horse made their way home through the deepening purple dusk.

Home was the Garden Glen Apartments, Unit 12.

Unit 12 was a very small apartment, which was just fine because Leroy was a very small man. Maybelline, however, was not a small horse. She was a tall horse and she was a wide horse, and she would not fit through the door of Unit 12.

"Gol' dang it," said Leroy Ninker.

He gave Maybelline a little push. And when that didn't work, he gave her a large shove. But Leroy soon saw that it was impossible. All the shoving in the world was not going to make Maybelline fit through the door of Unit 12.

"Dag blibber it," said Leroy. He actually felt like he might cry. Which was ridiculous because cowboys definitely did not cry.

Leroy closed his eyes, and Patty LeMarque's face floated into view. She opened her mouth and said, "Cogitate on item one if you care to move forward, Hank. You got to compliment the heck out of her!"

Leroy opened his eyes. He cleared his throat. He said, "Maybelline, you are the best squeeziest-into-a-small-spot horse that I have ever known."

Maybelline twitched her ears to the left and to the right, and while the horse was busy savoring the compliment, Leroy gave her a hopeful shove.

But Maybelline still wouldn't fit through the door.

"Flibber gibber it," said Leroy. He closed his eyes and conjured up Patty LeMarque's face again. He tried to remember the other items about Maybelline. He thought very hard.

"I got it," he said. "Item two is that you are the kind of horse who eats a lot of grub."

Leroy opened his eyes.

Maybelline was looking at him in an extremely hopeful manner.

"Well, yippie-i-okay," said Leroy Ninker. "I will make us some food, and then we will deal with the too-small door."

Maybelline looked as overjoyed as it was possible for a horse to look, and Leroy was moved to compliment her again.

"You are the most splendiferous horse in all of creation," he said.

Maybelline whinnied long and loud. She nodded in agreement.

She truly was an excellent horse.

Leroy didn't think he would ever be done admiring her.

Chapter Five

Leroy Ninker went into the kitchen of Unit 12. He opened the refrigerator and looked inside.

Leroy had viewed many, many Westerns at the Bijou Drive-In Theater. He had seen a great deal of purple mountains and wide-open plains. He had watched cowboys battling injustices and crossing rivers and eating beans.

But he could not recall one movie where a cowboy said aloud exactly what it was that he was feeding to his horse.

"Hay?" said Leroy. He lifted up his hat and scratched his head. "Oats?"

But he didn't have hay. And he didn't have oats.

"Dag flibber it," said Leroy Ninker.

Outside of Unit 12, Maybelline let out a long, loud whinny that had a question mark on the end of it.

"Okay!" Leroy shouted to the horse. "I am making you some grub! Yippie-i-oh."

Leroy grabbed a big pot and filled it with water. He turned the heat on high. He filled another pot with tomato sauce.

Patty LeMarque had said nothing about whether or not Maybelline liked spaghetti, but didn't everyone like spaghetti?

After Leroy Ninker added the noodles to the pot, he went outside and leaned up against his horse. Her flank was very warm. She was an extremely comforting horse to lean against.

Maybelline turned her head and looked at Leroy, and then she put her nose up in the air and sniffed.

"That's right," said Leroy. "I am cooking you some grub."

Maybelline whinnied.

"It's spaghetti," said Leroy. "I hope you like spaghetti."

It turned out that Maybelline did like spaghetti.

She liked a lot of spaghetti.

The horse ate the first pot of noodles in a single gigantic gulp. As far as Leroy could tell, she didn't even bother to chew.

When she was done, Maybelline lifted her head from the pot and looked at Leroy in a meaningful way. Leroy said, "Yippie-i-oh," and he went running back into Unit 12 with the empty pot and started boiling more water. He opened another jar of tomato sauce. He made a second pot of spaghetti.

After that, he made a third pot of spaghetti.

By the time Maybelline was done eating, the stars were shining in the sky and the moon was looking down and there was not one noodle of spaghetti left in Unit 12.

Leroy Ninker was very tired. He leaned against his horse and looked up at the stars. But when he closed his eyes, what he saw was Patty LeMarque. Her face was as big as the moon, and her mouth was opening and closing, and opening and closing.

Leroy knew exactly what she was saying.

Patty LeMarque was reciting item three.

"Maybelline?" said Leroy.

Maybelline turned and put her nose in Leroy's face.

"I have remembered item three," said Leroy Ninker. "Item three is that you are the kind of horse who gets lonesome quick."

Maybelline nickered.

"But you cannot fit inside Unit 12," said Leroy.

Maybelline shook her head.

"Okay, then," said Leroy. "I will stay here with you."

He took off his boots. He removed his lasso. He loosened his belt. And then he lay down at Maybelline's feet. He put his hat over his eyes. He sighed a happy sigh.

"I have made a lot of mistakes in my life," said Leroy Ninker from underneath his hat. "I have done some things that I wish I had not done. I have taken some wrong turns."

There was a long silence. Leroy moved his hat and looked up at Maybelline. The horse looked down at him. She was listening.

"There was a time in my life when I was a thief," said Leroy. "I am now reformed.

I hope you don't judge me, Maybelline, because I truly am a changed man."

Maybelline let out a small chuff of air.

"Oh, Maybelline," said Leroy. "You are my horse. For me, you shine brighter than every star and every planet. You shine brighter than all the universe's moons and suns. There are not enough *yippie-i-oh*s to describe you, Maybelline. I love you."

Leroy Ninker had never imagined that he could string so many words together at once. It was the longest speech of his life.

He looked up at Maybelline, and she looked down at him. Leroy's cheeks felt hot. He lowered his hat so that it covered his face. "Good night, Maybelline," he whispered.

Leroy closed his eyes. He thought very hard.

Had his heart been waiting for Maybelline to come along so that it could open wide and he could speak all the beautiful words that had been hiding inside of him?

It was an amazing concept to consider, and the cowboy fell asleep considering it.

Chapter Six

Leroy Ninker dreamed that he was riding Maybelline on the open plain. In the distance there were purple mountains, and high up in the sky there was a daytime moon. The moon was looking down at Leroy and Maybelline, and it was smiling at them.

In Leroy's dream, Maybelline was running very fast.

Also, she had a full set of teeth.

It's just like a movie, thought Leroy. *We are just like a horse and cowboy in a movie.*

The wind rushed across his face. It smelled like cinnamon and clover and spaghetti sauce.

The wind is promising me wonderful things, thought Leroy.

And then he thought, *Patty LeMarque is right. I am very good at speaking poeticals.*

Maybelline's hooves pounded on the earth.

Maybelline's hooves were extremely loud. Leroy had never heard such loud hooves, even in the movies. Maybelline's hooves were as loud as thunder.

The cinnamon-and-clover-and-spaghetti-sauce-scented wind blew harder and faster. It tickled Leroy's nostrils. And then it slapped him on the cheeks. The wind, obviously, was trying to tell Leroy something important.

And then, in his dream, Leroy heard Patty LeMarque's voice. "Wake up, Hank!" she shouted. "Protect your horse!"

Leroy Ninker woke up.

Thunder crashed. A bolt of lightning lit up the world.

"Dab blibber it," said Leroy. "It's fixing to rain." He stood. He hitched up his pants and pushed his hat down on his head. He looked at Maybelline. Her eyes were closed. She was still asleep.

"Horse of my heart," whispered Leroy, "sweetest and most delicate of all springtime blossoms, I cannot let you be rained on. I will go inside and get you an umbrella."

Maybelline's eyes stayed closed.

"I'll be right back," said Leroy.

He turned and ran into Unit 12.

While Leroy was gone, the rain began. A drop fell on Maybelline's nose. Another drop fell on her ear. The horse woke up. She lifted her head and looked around her.

Terrible things were happening!

Thunder was crashing!

Lightning was flashing!

And worst of all—oh, worst of all—Maybelline was utterly, absolutely alone.

She was not the kind of horse who liked to be alone.

Maybelline let out a long, questioning whinny. The thunder crashed; the lightning flashed. Maybelline called out again.

Where was the little man? Where was the little man with the big hat and the beautiful words? Where was the little man who brought her spaghetti?

Maybelline called out again and again. There was no answer.

She didn't know what to do. And when Maybelline didn't know what to do, what Maybelline did was run.

Leroy Ninker came out of Unit 12 holding an umbrella up high over his head. "Here I am, my springtime blossom," he said, "and I have brought you an umbrella."

But when he got to where Maybelline should be, there was no Maybelline there.

"Maybelline?" said Leroy into the darkness and the wind and the rain. "Maybelline?"

The wind blew harder.

"Horse of my heart?" said Leroy Ninker.

The rain came down hard and fast. The lightning flashed, revealing a horseless world.

Leroy stared into the emptiness. He heard Patty LeMarque's voice in the wind. She was saying, "Do not leave Maybelline alone for too long, or you will live to rue and regret the day."

A great gust of wind came along and grabbed hold of Leroy's umbrella and

ripped it right out of his hands. Leroy watched as the umbrella spun up into the darkness.

He was a cowboy without a horse, a cowboy without an umbrella. He was a cowboy absolutely, utterly alone.

Chapter Seven

The cowboy walked through the dark and stormy world, shouting, "Maybelline, Maybelline, Maybelline!"

In his haste to find his horse, Leroy had left Unit 12 without his boots and without his lasso. He was not at all prepared to go on a horse search, and he had no idea where to begin.

Patty LeMarque's face appeared before him and said, "Don't forget the compliments, Hank. And the grub."

"Maybelline!" Leroy shouted. "You are the queen of yippie-i-oh-ness! You are the most beautiful horse in all of creation."

No horse appeared.

"Maybelline!" Leroy shouted. "There will be unending pots of spaghetti if only you come home to me!"

No horse appeared.

Leroy thought about Maybelline and her bony spine and her four teeth. He considered her whiskered, velvety nose. He cogitated upon her twitching, twisting ears and how she bent her head down to listen to him. Oh, she listened to him so well.

"Maybelline," Leroy whispered into the darkness, "you are the horse for me."

The rain came down harder, and the wind blew meaner. Leroy's socks were soaked through.

This is the worst night of my life, thought Leroy. *If there is anything worse than being a cowboy without*

a horse, it is being a cowboy who had a horse and then lost her.

The wind howled and whistled. And then the wind grabbed hold of Leroy's hat and tossed it away.

"Dag blither it, you, you, *wind,* you . . ." Leroy shook his fist at the wind. "What am I going to do without my hat?"

Leroy Ninker was now hatless, bootless, lasso-less, and horseless.

He had never felt less like a cowboy.

"I want my horse!" Leroy Ninker shouted into the wind and rain. He sank to his knees. "Give me back my horse. Please, please. Maybelline, I promise that if I find you, I will never leave you alone again."

These words seemed so sad to Leroy that he started to cry. The wind blew stronger. The rain beat down. The world was very, very dark, and the cowboy was lost.

Oh, he was lost.

And where was the horse?

She was lost, too. She was as lost as she had ever been in her life. She was soaked to the hooves, and she was very afraid.

She was also tired.

She stopped running and held herself still in the darkness. She whinnied. And then she neighed. And then she nickered. Finally, she sighed.

The horse wanted many things. She wanted the rain to stop falling and the wind to stop howling. She wanted the little man to appear out of the darkness holding a gigantic pot of spaghetti.

But more than anything, Maybelline wanted to hear the little man's voice.

The horse needed to hear some beautiful words.

But there was no little man, and there were no beautiful words. There was just darkness and rain and wind. And since Maybelline couldn't think what to do, she started to run again. She ran without thinking or hoping.

* * *

In the darkness, the horse went one way.

And the cowboy, alas, went the other.

Chapter Eight

Leroy stood in a patch of mud. He looked down at his socks. They were very dirty. He looked up at the sky. He watched as the rain slowed to a trickle. The thunder grumbled and rumbled and then slunk away. The last raindrop fell. The world became very quiet.

The sky was gray, but at the horizon, there was the slightest hint of pink.

"Dawn is coming," said Leroy Ninker. "And I do not have a hat or boots or a lasso or a horse. I don't even have an umbrella. I have nothing at all."

Leroy watched the sun slowly rise; the orange ball of it glowed brighter and brighter. He shook his head sadly. He looked down at his muddy socks again.

And then, in the pink and hopeful light of dawn, Leroy noticed something in the dirt. He bent down and traced the shape that was imprinted in the mud. His heart thumped inside of him.

"Yippie-i-oh," whispered Leroy Ninker to the hoofprint.

He looked past the first hoofprint, and he saw there was a second one and then a third.

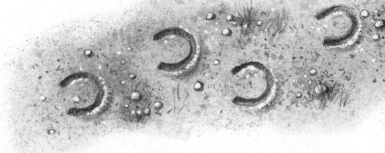

"Maybelline!" shouted Leroy Ninker.

He followed the hoofprints. He started to run. He may not have had a hat or a lasso or boots, but he was tracking a horse.

His horse.

Maybelline was out there somewhere. And a cowboy named Leroy Ninker would find her.

72

* * *

The horse was, indeed, out there somewhere. To be specific, she was three streets
over. The horse was on Deckawoo Drive.

She was standing at the window of a
house. She was watching a family sitting
down to breakfast. Wonderful, wonderful
smells were coming from inside the house,
and the family looked happy sitting together
around the table. Maybelline put her nose

very close to the window. She watched the family. She admired the food.

And when she could not bear it any longer, she raised her head and called out. She whinnied long and loud.

Leroy Ninker was following the hoofprints when he heard a sound that made him stop in his tracks. Leroy held himself very still. He listened.

He heard birdsong and the low hum of a train. He heard the whoosh of car tires on the wet pavement.

And then he heard that beautiful, singular noise again: *a whinny.* A horse. His horse. Maybelline.

Leroy ran in the direction of the whinny.

"Maybelline!" he called out. "I am on my way!"

He leaped over a bush. He ran around a bicycle. He climbed over a fence and into a backyard.

And there was Maybelline! She was standing and looking in the window of a house.

"Maybelline!" shouted Leroy.

The horse turned and looked at him. She twisted her ears left and right. Both ears trembled hopefully. It was obvious that she was waiting for some beautiful words.

Leroy's throat felt tight.

He smiled. He spread his arms wide. "Horse of my heart," he called out, "most wondrous, most glorious of all horses, I have missed you so."

Maybelline nickered. She came trotting toward him.

Leroy put his arms around her. He closed his eyes and leaned his head against her neck.

He had done it. He had taken hold of fate with both hands and wrestled it to the ground. And he had done it without a lasso, without boots, without a hat.

"Oh, Maybelline," said Leroy Ninker. "I have so many words I want to say to you."

Leroy's eyes were still closed when he heard a voice say, "Mister, is that your horse?"

Chapter Nine

Leroy Ninker opened his eyes. He saw a small girl.

"Is it?" she said. "Is that your horse?"

"Yes," said Leroy Ninker. "This is my horse. She was lost, and I tracked her through the mud. She was lost, and I found her."

"Uh-huh. What's her name?"

"Maybelline," said Leroy.

"My name is Stella," said the girl. "Can I pet your horse?"

"Yes," said Leroy Ninker. "But what this horse really likes is a compliment. Do you know how to give a compliment?"

"Of course I do," said Stella. She put her hand on Maybelline's nose. She looked Maybelline in the eye and said, "You are a very nice-looking horse. You are the nicest-looking horse I have ever seen. Of course, I have never seen a horse before. But I have seen a pig. There is a pig who lives on this street. I know that pigs and horses are not the same at all. Other than that they both have hooves. Even though they are different kinds of hooves. You have very nice hooves, by the way."

Maybelline twitched her ears this way and that. She let out a pleased-sounding chuff of air.

"Stella!" shouted a boy. "Stella, watch out. Horses can be very dangerous. They can kick out suddenly with their hind legs and harm the unsuspecting."

"That's my brother, Frank," said Stella to Leroy. "He worries a lot."

Maybelline put her nose up in the air. She sniffed. She whinnied and put a question mark at the end of the whinny.

"What you are smelling is toast," said Stella to Maybelline. "Every morning, Mrs. Watson makes toast for her pig. Mercy is the name of the pig, and she is a pig who likes toast with a great deal of butter on it. Have you ever had toast with a great deal of butter on it? It's very good."

"Wait a minute," said Leroy Ninker. "Is this Deckawoo Drive?"

"This is Deckawoo Drive," said Stella.

"I have been here before," said Leroy.

And just as Leroy Ninker finished saying these words, a woman stepped out on the front porch of the house next door.

She was holding a butter knife in her hand, and a pig was standing beside her.

"Good morning, Stella," called the woman. "And Mr. Ninker! It is lovely to see you again."

"Hello, Mrs. Watson," said Leroy Ninker. "I would like for you to meet my horse, Maybelline."

"Well," said Mrs. Watson, "what a wonderful horse. She looks like a true equine wonder. You must both come inside and have some toast."

"But I don't know if Maybelline will fit through the door," said Leroy.

"Oh, heavens," said Mrs. Watson. "There is always a way to make things fit. Come inside, come inside."

"Come on," said Stella. She took hold
of Leroy's hand.

Leroy turned to his horse. He said,
"Come with me, horse of my heart. We
are going to eat some toast."

The cowboy started to walk.

The horse followed along behind him.

The cowboy and the horse went inside.

Coda

Every evening, Leroy rode Maybelline to work. Maybelline stood beside the Bijou Drive-In Theater concession stand. She watched the movies. She ate popcorn.

Maybelline liked all the movies. She was particularly delighted when a horse showed up in a movie. Or a cowboy.

But Maybelline's favorite movies were the love stories. She put her ears up in the air and listened very closely to the beautiful words that people said to each other. As they spoke, she nodded and nickered quietly.

The horse was happy.

She knew that late at night, on the way home from the Bijou, Leroy would speak to her. Word after beautiful word would come from the cowboy's mouth, from his heart.

And in the darkness, underneath the bright stars, Maybelline would listen to them all.

For Lisa Beck, who is good in every crisis
K. D.

To my friends Dave and Terri, with love
C. V.

Tales from Deckawoo Drive

Volume Two

Francine Poulet Meets the Ghost Raccoon

Chapter One

Francine Poulet was an animal control officer.

She hailed from a long line of animal control officers.

Francine's father, Clement Poulet, had been an animal control officer, and Francine's grandmother Nanette Poulet had been an animal control officer, too.

Francine had won many animal control trophies—forty-seven of them, to be exact.

In addition, Francine was the Gizzford County record holder for most animals controlled. She had successfully and officially and expeditiously (for the most part) captured dogs, cats, rats, pigs, snakes, squirrels, chipmunks, bats, raccoons, and, also, fish.

One time, Francine had faced down a bear. The bear and Francine had stared at each other for a long time.

The bear blinked first.

Francine Poulet was an excellent animal control officer.

She was never, ever afraid.

Late one afternoon in May, the phone at the Animal Control Center rang.

Francine Poulet was sitting at her desk. She answered the phone. She said, "Animal Control Officer Francine Poulet here. How may I help you?"

"Yes, hello," said the voice at the other end. "Mrs. Bissinger speaking."

"Uh-huh," said Francine.

"I am being tormented," said Mrs. Bissinger.

"Yep," said Francine.

Everyone who called the Animal Control Center was being tormented in one way or another. Francine was never surprised to hear about it.

Nothing frightened Francine Poulet, and nothing surprised her either.

"A most unusual raccoon has come to reside on my roof," said Mrs. Bissinger.

100

"Right," said Francine. "Raccoon on the roof. What's your address?"

"Perhaps you were not listening," said Mrs. Bissinger. "This is not your average raccoon."

"Right," said Francine, "not your average raccoon." She leaned back in her chair. And then she leaned back a bit farther.

Francine leaned back so far that the front legs of the chair lifted off the ground. This was a bad habit of Francine's. Her father, Clement Poulet, had tried to break her of it, but he had never succeeded.

"One of these days, Franny," her father used to say, "you are going to tip all the way backwards in that chair and whack your head, and then you will be sorry."

Clement Poulet was dead, and it been many years since he had warned his daughter about chair-tipping. Francine missed Clement. She even missed his dire predictions. However, she had yet to tip all the way backward and whack her head. Francine had been gifted with an extraordinary sense of balance.

"This raccoon," said Mrs. Bissinger, "shimmers."

"He what?" said Francine.

"Shimmers," said Mrs. Bissinger. "He seems to glow. In addition, and more disturbingly, this raccoon calls my name."

Francine slowly lowered the chair legs to the floor.

"Interesting," said Francine. "The raccoon says, 'Mrs. Bissinger'?"

"No," said Mrs. Bissinger. "He says 'Tammy.' He screams my first name. He screams it like a banshee. Perhaps this raccoon is a ghost raccoon?"

"There are no ghosts," said Francine Poulet. "And there are no ghosts of raccoons."

"Be that as it may," said Mrs. Bissinger, "there is a shimmery raccoon on my roof who calls my name. And so on."

"Right," said Francine. "The address?"

"Forty-two fourteen Fleeker Street," said Mrs. Bissinger.

"I'll see you tonight," said Francine.

"Bring a ladder," said Mrs. Bissinger. "The roof is very steep and very high. You are not afraid of heights, are you?"

"I am not afraid of anything," said Francine.

"How inspiring," said Mrs. Bissinger. "I look forward to making your acquaintance."

"And I look forward to catching your raccoon," said Francine. She hung up the phone. She leaned back in her chair and studied her trophies, all forty-seven of them. She started to hum.

Francine's father had always told her that she was like a refrigerator.

What he said exactly was, "Franny, you are the genuine article. You are solid.

You are certain. You are like a refrigerator. You hum."

Francine leaned back in her chair. She balanced the chair on two legs.

"A talking ghost raccoon?" she said. "I don't think so."

She hummed louder. She leaned back farther.

"Watch out, Mr. Raccoon," said Francine Poulet. "I am going to get you."

Chapter Two

That night, Francine Poulet drove her
animal control truck to 4214 Fleeker
Street. She rang the doorbell.

A woman wearing a large diamond
necklace, dangly ruby earrings, several
flashy rings, and a multi-stone brooch
answered the door.

Francine squinted.

"Mrs. Bissinger?" she said.

"Exactly," said Mrs. Bissinger. "Tammy Bissinger. How do you do?"

"I do just fine," said Francine. "I am here about your raccoon."

"I assumed," said Mrs. Bissinger. She stood there glittering. "And so on," she said.

"Well," said Francine, "okay, then. I think I will just head up on the roof and catch this raccoon."

"You will find him to be a wily adversary, almost supernatural in his abilities," said Mrs. Bissinger.

"Uh-huh," said Francine.

"He insists on saying my name," said Mrs. Bissinger.

"Yep," said Francine. "You told me that."

"Has a raccoon ever said your name?"

"Nope," said Francine. She turned her back on Mrs. Bissinger and headed to the truck.

She unloaded her ladder. She retrieved her net. She checked her flashlight for batteries. And then Francine put the ladder against the side of the house. She turned the flashlight on and put it between her teeth. She grasped the net firmly in one hand and a rung of the ladder firmly in the other.

Francine Poulet started to climb.

As she climbed, she hummed.

She was solid. She was certain. She was Animal Control Officer Francine Poulet.

At the top of the ladder, Francine stepped out onto the roof. She took the flashlight out of her mouth. She turned and shone it back on the ground, and there was Mrs. Bissinger, standing and looking up at her, all her jewelry twinkling and glowing.

"Be careful!" shouted Mrs. Bissinger. "He is an extraordinary raccoon! He shimmers! He screams like a banshee! And so on!"

"Right," said Francine. "Yep. Yep. You told me. He shimmers. He screams like a banshee. Got it."

Francine turned off the flashlight.

The thing about catching wild animals is not to let them smell your fear.

Since Francine Poulet was never, ever afraid, this was not a problem for her.

The other thing about catching wild animals is that the more you chase them, the faster they run.

It is best to let the wild ones come to you.

Francine sat down on the roof. She stretched her arms and legs. She cracked her knuckles. She hummed.

"What are you doing?" shouted Mrs. Bissinger from down below.

Francine ignored her.

It was pleasant, sitting on the roof in the dark, ignoring Mrs. Bissinger.

Francine hummed louder.

"Oh, Mr. Raccoon," whispered Francine, "everything is perfectly fine. There is no one here except for you and me, and we are friendly friends, you and me."

Francine closed her eyes. She hummed some more.

She heard a footfall. And then another footfall.

Francine smiled a very big smile without opening her eyes. She kept humming. Slowly, slowly she reached out and put her hand on the animal control net.

And then there came a high-pitched scream.

It did not sound like the raccoon was saying "Tammy."

Instead, it sounded like this: *"Frannnnnnnnnnyyyyy!"*

Francine couldn't believe it. The raccoon was saying her name.

She opened her eyes just in time to see a shimmery, raccoon-shaped object flying through the air. It was headed directly for her.

"Frannnnnnnnnyyyyyyyyyy!" screamed the ghost raccoon.

Animal Control Officer Francine Poulet, daughter of Animal Control Officer Clement Poulet, granddaughter of Animal Control Officer Nanette Poulet, was, for the first time in her life, afraid. In fact, she was terrified.

Chapter Three

The raccoon was running straight toward Francine. His teeth were bared, and they did not look like ghost teeth. They looked like raccoon teeth.

"Frannnnnnnnnyyyyyyyyyy!" screamed the raccoon.

Francine Poulet dropped her net. "Aaaaack!" she screamed back.

Francine's heart was beating so fast that she thought it might actually leap out of her chest and skitter across the roof.

She started to run.

She could feel the raccoon at her heels. She could smell his breath, and it did not smell good.

Where was the ladder? Where had she left it? She couldn't think.

"*Frannnnnnyyyyyyyyyyyy!*" screamed the raccoon.

No one in Francine's life had ever called her "Franny" except for her father.

How did the raccoon know to call her secret name?

Was the raccoon truly a ghost?

These were exactly the kinds of questions that Francine did not think she should be considering at this juncture.

She looked around her wildly. She spotted the ladder. She ran toward it. She had one foot on the ladder and one on the roof when she heard Mrs. Bissinger's disembodied voice say, "Have you captured the raccoon?"

"What?" shouted Francine.

"Frannnnnnnyyyyyyyyyyyy!" screamed the raccoon.

"The raccoon," said Mrs. Bissinger. "Have you captured him?"

"Forget the raccoon," said Francine. "I am trying to save my life here."

"How disappointing," said Mrs. Bissinger. "And so on."

120

Francine started to climb down the ladder.

"I told you he was *not* an ordinary raccoon," said Mrs. Bissinger's extremely annoying voice. There was a long pause. Mrs. Bissinger cleared her throat. "But then, I had heard that you were not an ordinary animal control officer."

Something about this comment stopped Francine. Mrs. Bissinger was right. Francine Poulet was not an ordinary animal control officer. She was the owner of forty-seven trophies. She was the proud holder of the Gizzford County record for most animals controlled. What was she doing running from a raccoon just because he was screaming "Frannnnnnnnnyyyyyyyyyyyy"?

Francine started to climb back up the ladder.

"How inspiring," said Mrs. Bissinger. "How truly inspiring. Back into battle. And so on."

Francine got to the top of the ladder. She put one foot on the roof and then the other foot. She crouched. She waited. Everything was very silent. Francine could hear her heart beating. She was afraid. She knew that it was dangerous to be afraid. But she wasn't sure how, exactly, to *stop* being afraid.

"Mr. Raccoon?" whispered Francine.

The raccoon answered her. He answered her by screaming his terrible scream and by bounding out of the darkness and throwing himself directly at her.

The raccoon hit Francine with such tremendous, raccoon-y force that she lost her balance and fell forward.

"Oooof," said Francine.

Not knowing what else to do, she grabbed hold of the raccoon. She wrapped her arms around him.

He didn't *feel* like a ghost. He felt extremely solid. He smelled like a dirty winter coat.

Also, he was very loud.

He kept screaming.

Actually, there was a lot of screaming. Someone else was screaming, too. Who was it?

It was Francine Poulet who was screaming!

How embarrassing, thought Francine.

But still, she couldn't seem to stop.

She and the raccoon were rolling around together and they were both screaming, and then, somehow, she and the raccoon were falling.

They were falling together, and they were falling for what seemed like a very long time.

Francine thought, *Mrs. Bissinger is right. This is a very tall roof.*

And then Animal Control Officer Francine Poulet hit the ground.

Everything went dark.

129

Chapter Four

Francine Poulet woke up in a hospital bed. Her left leg was in a cast, and her right arm was in a cast. Her neck was in a brace. Her head hurt.

"I am solid as a refrigerator," said Francine out loud.

These words didn't sound very believable.

"I am Animal Control Officer Francine Poulet," said Francine.

These words didn't sound very believable either.

She sniffed. She smelled cigar smoke.

"Over here, Franny," she heard someone say.

Francine turned her head very, very slowly and saw that her father was standing beside her bed.

"Pop?" she said.

"The one and only," said Clement Poulet.

"Aren't you dead?" said Francine.

"Absolutely," said her father.

"Oh," said Francine.

Clement Poulet puffed on his cigar. He blew the smoke into the air above Francine's bed.

"What were you doing up there, Franny?" he said.

"Up where?" said Francine.

"Up on the roof," said Clement Poulet.

"I was trying to catch that raccoon," said Francine.

"You panicked, though, didn't you?" said her father.

"I thought that raccoon knew my name. I thought that maybe the raccoon was a ghost."

"Pooh," said Clement Poulet, "that raccoon was nothing but a screamer. There aren't ghost raccoons, Franny. You know that."

Francine nodded, even though it hurt her head to nod. She knew there were no ghost raccoons. Of course she knew that.

"Also," said Clement Poulet, "Poulets do not panic. Even in the face of screaming raccoons."

Francine nodded. She knew that, too.

"It will be okay, Franny," said Clement Poulet.

"Will it?" she said. She felt a single tear roll out of her left eye and down her cheek. Francine missed her father telling her that everything was going to be okay. A tear rolled out of her right eye. And then tears fell from both eyes. Francine gave herself over to crying. After a while, she fell asleep.

When she woke up, her father was gone and Mrs. Bissinger was sitting in a chair beside the bed. She was wearing all her jewelry and she was holding a copy of the

Gizzford Gazette. The front-page headline read:

Below the headline, there was a picture of Francine Poulet taken at the previous year's awards banquet. She was holding a trophy (number 47) and smiling a very large smile.

Underneath the picture were the words "Raccoon Still at Large; Animal Control Officer Poulet Recuperating at the Gizzford Regional Hospital."

"They call that a tumble?" said Francine. "I fell three stories."

"Oh, good," said Mrs. Bissinger, "you're awake. Shall I read you the entire article?"

"No," said Francine. Her left foot, the one in the cast, itched.

"Can you scratch my left foot?" she said to Mrs. Bissinger.

Mrs. Bissinger put down the paper and stood up and gave Francine's foot a tentative little tap.

"How's that?" she said.

"That didn't help at all," said Francine.

"Oh, well," said Mrs. Bissinger. "I've never been much good at scratching people's feet." She picked up the paper and sat back down.

"It says here that your father was an animal control officer," said Mrs. Bissinger from behind the paper.

"That's true," said Francine.

"It says here," said Mrs. Bissinger, "that you are the most decorated animal control officer in the history of Gizzford."

"That's true, too," said Francine.

Mrs. Bissinger lowered the paper. She looked Francine in the eye. She said, "Yet you failed to capture my raccoon."

"Yes," said Francine. "I failed. I panicked." She turned her head and looked out the window. It was dark outside. Francine could see the lights of Gizzford winking and blinking, mocking her.

"Well," said Mrs. Bissinger, "your leg will heal and your arm will heal and you

138

will exit the hospital and you will continue in the world. You will find a way to continue in spite of your failure, I suppose. And so on."

"No," said Francine.

"Beg pardon?" said Mrs. Bissinger.

"No," said Francine. "There will be no 'and so on.' I quit."

"What?" said Mrs. Bissinger.

"I quit," said Francine. "I am no longer Animal Control Officer Francine Poulet."

Chapter Five

Time passed.

First the cast came off Francine's arm, and then the cast came off her leg. Francine walked with a limp and a cane. Sometimes her leg ached. Sometimes her arm ached.

But she was healed, sort of.

And so, early one morning in September, Francine walked into the Animal Control Center and turned in her uniform.

"What is the meaning of this?" said Mordus Toopher, chairman of the board of the Animal Control Center.

Mordus Toopher wore a brown corduroy suit and a brown-and-orange toupee. The toupee had always disturbed Francine. It reminded her of a chipmunk pelt.

"I quit," said Francine.

"What are you saying to me?" said Mordus. He adjusted his chipmunk toupee.

"I'm saying I quit," said Francine.

"You have battled many a snake and outwitted many a squirrel," said Mordus. "You have stared a bear, that dark and ferocious mystery, in the eye, and that dark and ferocious mystery blinked first."

"True," said Francine.

"And now you have reached this impasse of the soul, this gloomy, doomy time of self-appraisal. I wonder: Will you dwell here in your small shame and sad defeat? Will you truly allow yourself to be undone by one ignoble screaming raccoon?"

"Yes," said Francine.

Mordus Toopher shook his head. His toupee slipped a little. "Unbelievable," he said. He shook his head again. He righted his toupee.

"I am deeply saddened," he said. "Deeply saddened, yes. It is the end of an era. It is the end of an era that began with Nanette Poulet and continued with Clement Poulet and now it ends; it ends. The era ends with a dull, inharmonious thud. It ends with Francine and a raccoon."

"Can I have my trophies?" said Francine.

"I am afraid that the trophies must remain here," said Mordus, "property of Gizzford Animal Control Center, procured under the auspices, et cetera, et cetera. And et cetera." He smiled a sad smile.

"Right," said Francine. "Okay. Well, thanks for all the good times."

Mordus Toopher raised his right hand and waved good-bye. "The end of an era," he said. "The end."

Francine Poulet walked out of the Animal Control Center. She did not look back.

But that evening, Francine limped down to Fleeker Street and hid in a rhododendron bush. She studied Mrs. Bissinger's house.

She watched the dusk turn into a velvety darkness. She watched as a gibbous moon rose in the sky and shone on Mrs. Bissinger's empty, extremely tall, extremely steep roof.

There was no raccoon in sight.

"You weren't even a ghost," said Francine to the empty roof. "You were just a raccoon. I panicked. And Poulets never panic."

"Why are you hiding in my rhododendron?" said a voice.

Francine looked up. Mrs. Bissinger was standing above her, bejeweled and gleaming.

146

"I am not hiding," said Francine. "And so on."

"And so on," agreed Mrs. Bissinger. She sighed. She twinkled. "It is time to move on, Francine. The raccoon is gone. You must go, too."

"Okay," said Francine.

Mrs. Bissinger walked away. Francine continued to crouch in the rhododendron bush. She looked away from the roof, up into the dark sky. She could see some stars, but not many. Shouldn't there be more stars? The world seemed very dark.

Her arm ached. And her heart. Francine's heart ached, too.

She didn't know who she was. She was not an animal control officer. And she was not a Poulet, because Poulets never panic.

"Who am I?" said Francine to the dark sky.

There was no answer.

"Tell me who I am!" shouted Francine.

And then, from somewhere far away, there came an answer.

"Go home, Francine!"

Francine looked up. Mrs. Bissinger was standing in a lighted window. "Go home!" she shouted again. She waved her arms around.

Francine stood up. She exited the rhododendron bush. She went home.

Chapter Six

Francine Poulet got a job as a cashier at Clyde's Bait, Feed, Tackle, and Animal Necessities.

Her left leg, the one she had broken when she fell from Mrs. Bissinger's roof with the raccoon in her arms, continued to ache. So Francine sat on a stool as she rang up dog chow and plastic worms, chicken feed and rawhide bones, fishing poles and horse bridles.

For some reason, Clyde's Bait, Feed, Tackle, and Animal Necessities was bedeviled by flies. Francine kept a fly swatter on hand at all times. She got very good at whacking flies.

Other than the flies, it was a quiet existence.

There were no emergency calls. There were no dramatic chases. There were no raccoons who called her name. There was no Mrs. Bissinger. And so on.

Clement Poulet did not show up in the brightly lit aisles of Clyde's. There was no smell of cigar smoke. There was no suggestion that Francine was disappointing anyone or that she was not as solid as a refrigerator.

Also, a stool was not a chair. It was very, very hard to tip backward on the legs of a stool. Francine did not even try. It seemed too dangerous.

Francine sat. The days passed.

She rang up a lot of dog chow.

She killed a lot of flies. In fact, she kept a running tally of how many flies she had whacked, just so she could convince herself that she was making progress of some sort.

On the day that Francine killed her 238th fly, a girl and a boy came into Clyde's Bait, Feed, Tackle, and Animal Necessities.

The girl said, "Where are your sweets?"

"We don't deal in sweets," said Francine Poulet.

She could hear Fly 239 buzzing at her ear.

"Not even licorice?" said the girl.

"No licorice," said Francine.

Fly 239 zoomed back and forth in front of her, taunting her.

"Hey," said the boy, "I know you."

Francine took her eyes off the fly and looked at the boy.

"My name is Frank," he said.

"Good for you," said Francine.

"And you are Animal Control Officer Francine Poulet," said Frank. "Once you were on official business on our street. Also, I saw your picture in the paper."

"What about cough drops?" said the girl. "Do you have cough drops? Sometimes when a store doesn't sell candy, they will sell cough drops."

"Stella," said Frank, "there aren't any sweets here."

"That just doesn't seem right to me," said Stella. "That seems wrong. How can you run a store without selling sweets?"

"You are a highly decorated animal control officer," said Frank to Francine. "You are from a long line of animal control officers."

Francine's toes felt funny. Her stomach was squiffy.

"Why are you working here?" said Frank.

"That's none of your beeswax," said Francine. She swung the fly swatter through the air in a menacing sort of way, even though Fly 239 had disappeared.

"You fell off a roof with a raccoon in your arms," said Frank. "You took a tumble."

"It was not a tumble," said Francine. "It was way more than a tumble."

"I read about it in the paper," said Frank.

"Frank reads the whole paper. He reads it from back to front," said Stella. "He reads every word of it, and he remembers it all. That's what Frank does. That's the way he is."

"I pay attention," said Frank.

"He worries," said Stella.

"The raccoon got away," said Frank. "And the raccoon that got away is a screamer."

Francine's toes twitched. Her heart thumped.

Clement Poulet had called the raccoon a screamer, too.

157

"So?" said Francine. "So what?"

"So, I know where your screaming raccoon is," said Frank.

Chapter Seven

"He is not my raccoon," said Francine. "He is on the roof of the Lincoln Sisters' house. I have heard him and I have seen him. I have watched him through my binoculars. I own a very good pair of binoculars."

"Good for you, kid," said Francine Poulet.

"I keep an eye and an ear on things on Deckawoo Drive," said Frank.

"He worries," said Stella.

"Deckawoo Drive?" said Francine. "I once caught a pig on Deckawoo Drive."

"That's Mercy Watson!" said Stella. "She likes to eat toast with a great deal of butter on it."

"Raccoons carry rabies," said Frank. "Raccoons bite. Raccoons steal things. I read an article about a raccoon who stole a baby right out of its cradle."

"What?" said Stella.

"It's true," said Frank.

"What was the baby's name?" said Stella.

"That is an unimportant detail," said Frank. "The important thing is that it happened. Raccoons are dangerous."

RACCOON STEALS BABY

Francine felt her toes curling up. Her arm ached. Her leg ached. Fly 239 flew by. Francine looked down at her hands. They were shaking.

"You're afraid," said Frank.

"I am not afraid," said Francine.

"Yes, you are," said Frank. "Your hands are shaking. That is a sign of fear."

"I'm not well," said Francine. "I don't feel good."

"You're never going to feel good until you face that raccoon," said Frank.

"Get out of here, kid," said Francine. She swung her fly swatter in the direction of the door.

"What would your father say?" said Frank.

"What?" said Francine. She felt her heart skitter and stutter inside of her.

"Your father. Animal Control Officer Clement Poulet."

"You didn't know my father," said Francine.

"No," said Frank. "I did not. But I read about him. He was a very brave man, and in the article in the paper, it said that he was proud of you."

Francine stared at Frank.

Frank stared at Francine.

Stella sighed a deep sigh. "You know what I wish? I wish we could go someplace where they sell sweets. I wish we could go to a place where they sell jelly beans or chocolate-covered peanuts or gumdrops. I love gumdrops."

"You were an outstanding animal control officer once," said Frank.

"I was," said Francine. "I was one of the greats. And then I panicked. Poulets do not panic." She stared down at the fly swatter in her trembling hands.

"Maybe you are still a great animal control officer," said Frank. "Why don't you find out? Come to Deckawoo Drive and help us capture the raccoon."

Frank took hold of Stella's hand. "Come on, Stella," he said. "We'll go and get you some sweets."

Frank and Stella left Clyde's Bait, Feed, Tackle, and Animal Necessities.

Francine sat on her stool. Fly 239 buzzed around her head. A great shaft of sunlight came in through the plate-glass windows of Clyde's and made the bags of dog chow glow like misshapen ghosts.

Frank's words echoed in Francine's head. *Maybe you are still a great animal control officer.*

Maybe.

Could it be true?

The door to Clyde's opened, and Stella walked in.

"Close your eyes and hold out your hand," said Stella.

Francine Poulet closed her eyes and held out her hand. She felt a small tickle in the center of her palm.

"Okay," said Stella. "You can look now."

Francine looked down. In her hand was a gumdrop, a green one.

"You should come and get the raccoon," said Stella. "It would make Frank happy. He worries."

After Stella left Clyde's Bait, Feed, Tackle, and Animal Necessities, Francine put the gumdrop in her mouth. It tasted sweet.

Francine rocked her stool back and forth. She felt one leg of it lift the tiniest bit off the floor.

And Francine Poulet made a small noise that sounded almost like a hum.

Chapter Eight

Former Animal Control Officer Francine Poulet stood in the darkness on Deckawoo Drive.

She held a net. Her hands were trembling. The net was moving up and down and swaying back and forth.

Frank was standing at Francine's side.

"Shhhhh," said Frank.

"I didn't say anything," said Francine. The net bounced up and down.

Frank handed Francine the binoculars.

"Look," he said. "Is that your raccoon?"

Francine put the net on the ground. She took the binoculars. She held them up and looked through them. She saw the raccoon sitting on the roof, staring at her.

The moon was bright, and it was shining on the raccoon's fur. The raccoon shimmered.

"Eeep," said Francine.

"What?" said Frank.

"That is the raccoon," said Francine. "That is him. He is that. Oh, oh, oh. Whoop. Eep."

"Calm down," said Frank.

"I'm afraid," said Francine.

Frank took hold of her hand.

"That doesn't help," said Francine.

Frank squeezed her hand very hard. "Okay," said Francine. "Maybe it helps a little."

"This is the plan, Miss Poulet," said Frank. "I will hold the ladder. And you will climb up it, and you will take your net with you. You will capture the raccoon with your net, just as you have captured other raccoons with your net. Remember, you have forty-seven trophies."

"Forty-seven," said Francine in a voice of wonder.

"You got into a staring contest with a bear and you won," said Frank.

"I did?" said Francine.

"You did," said Frank. "Climb the ladder, Miss Poulet."

"Okay," said Francine. "I will climb now."

Francine grabbed hold of the ladder. She took a step up and then another step up. She tried to hum, but she couldn't remember how. Suddenly, humming seemed like a very complicated thing.

"Just climb," whispered Frank.

So Francine climbed. She climbed some more.

And suddenly, there she was, standing on the roof, her whole body trembling like a tiny leaf in a ferocious November wind.

From somewhere on the roof, the raccoon screamed.

"Miss Poulet?" said Frank.

"Yes?" said Francine.

"Be brave," said Frank.

"Okay," said Francine. She sat down. She put her head between her knees.

"Miss Poulet?" said Frank. "Miss Poulet?"

And then from down below came another voice. The other voice said, "Franklin Endicott, I would like it very much if you explained yourself."

"There is a raccoon on your roof, Miss Lincoln," said Frank. "And I have arranged for the best animal control officer in the county, in the country, maybe even in the entire world, to catch your raccoon. That animal control officer is on your roof right now."

A door slammed. "Sister!" said a different voice. "Are you all right?"

"Most certainly not! Some strange woman is on our roof."

Francine raised her head from her knees. She peered over the edge of the roof. There were two old women in bathrobes staring up at her.

One of the women waved. She said, "Hello, my name is Baby. And this is my sister, Eugenia."

"We're not at a garden party, Baby," said Eugenia. "There is no need to introduce yourself."

"And who are you?" said Baby to Francine.

"Um," said Francine. Her stomach felt squiffy.

"Are you truly an animal control officer?" shouted Eugenia. "Or are you just some nut job gallivanting on my roof? And more to the point, who says I have a raccoon on my roof to begin with?"

"Oh, but Sister," said Baby Lincoln, "we do have a raccoon living on our roof. I have seen him many times. And I have thought it would be wonderful if we could name him."

"Name him?" said Eugenia. "*Name* him?"

A door banged open. A woman shouted, "Frank? Eugenia? Baby? Is everything okay?"

"Hello, Mrs. Watson," said Frank. "Everything is fine. There is a raccoon on the Lincoln Sisters' roof, and we are in the process of capturing it."

"Are you sure it's a raccoon?" said Mrs. Watson. "It looks like a woman."

178

"That's Animal Control Officer Francine Poulet," said Frank.

"Oh," said Mrs. Watson. "Of course. I didn't recognize her in the dark. Hello, dear. You once helped us locate our porcine wonder. Hello."

And then, in the middle of this slightly inane exchange of pleasantries, there came a terrible, bloodcurdling scream.

"Frannnnnnnnnnnnnnnnnnnyyyyyyyyyyyyyyyyyyy!"

Chapter Nine

Francine shivered. She trembled.

The raccoon screamed again.

"What a rude noise," said Eugenia.

"It is just the raccoon," said Baby. "He screams. Have you never heard him scream before, Sister?"

"No," said Eugenia. "I have never heard him scream before. I am too busy to listen for screaming raccoons."

"Frannnnnnnnnnyyyyy!" screamed the raccoon.

"I think he is lonely!" said Baby.

"For heaven's sake, Baby," said Eugenia, "the raccoon is not lonely."

Francine's heart skittered and skipped and thumped. She stayed crouched on the roof.

"That animal control woman is worthless," said Eugenia. "She is doing absolutely nothing."

"I must say that she was very helpful when Mercy went missing," said Mrs. Watson.

"She looks like a fraud to me," said Eugenia.

"She is not a fraud," said Frank. "She is the genuine article."

The genuine article!

Those were the words that Francine's father had used. That was exactly what Clement Poulet had said: You are the genuine article, Franny.

"Raaaaaaaaaaannnnnnnyyyyyy!" screamed the raccoon.

Francine listened closely.

What was the raccoon saying?

"Grannnnnnnnnnnnnnnnnnnnnnnyyyy!" he screamed.

Why, he was saying absolutely nothing.

The raccoon did not know her name.

The raccoon was just screaming a scream. That was all.

Francine looked down at her hands on the net. They were not shaking. She was not trembling.

And why was that?

It was because she was the genuine article.

It was because she was as solid as a refrigerator.

It was because she was Francine Poulet.

Francine stood up.

"I am Animal Control Officer Francine Poulet!" she shouted. "I am the daughter of Animal Control Officer Clement Poulet and the granddaughter of Animal Control Officer Nanette Poulet."

"That's right," said Frank.

Annnnnnnnnnnnnnnnnnyyyyyyyy! screamed the raccoon.

"I am the genuine article!" shouted Francine.

"Yes, you are," said Frank.

"What a lot of nonsense this is," said Eugenia. "Why don't you just do something?"

"I am now going to capture the raccoon!" shouted Francine.

184

"That is a really good idea, Miss Poulet," said Frank, "because the raccoon is standing right beside you."

Francine looked down.

Frank was exactly right. The raccoon was standing right beside her.

She looked at him. He looked at her. He bared his teeth. Francine bared her teeth back. She was not afraid. She was not one bit afraid.

Slowly, confidently, Francine raised the animal control net and lowered it over the raccoon.

Just like that.

"Kid?" said Francine.

"Yes, Miss Poulet?" said Frank.

"Get the cage ready, kid. I have captured the raccoon."

"I'm on it, Miss Poulet."

"I wonder if anyone is hungry," said Mrs. Watson from down below. "I wonder if I should make some toast."

And up on the roof, Francine Poulet started to hum.

Coda

Francine was reinstated by Mordus Toopher.

Mordus Toopher said, "This is a day of reclamation. This is a day when the shadows recede and the sun shines brightly. The true self is recalled and celebrated, and the trophies are returned to the animal control officer both literally and metaphorically. What I mean to say is: welcome back, Francine."

"Thank you, sir," said Francine. "I am happy to be back."

"And who is this young and earnest fellow?" said Mordus Toopher.

"My name is Franklin Endicott, sir," said Frank. "I am Miss Poulet's understudy. If you don't mind."

"Mind?" said Mordus Toopher. "How could I mind? Who would object to the passing on of such skill and knowledge? It is the beginning of an era. I applaud you."

"Me?" said Frank.

"Both of you," said Mordus Toopher. "I applaud both of you." He adjusted his toupee. "Happy, meaningful, and productive days are ahead, I'm sure."

◆ ◆ ◆

Francine and Frank rode together in the animal control truck.

Sometimes, in the purple light of early evening, Frank would say, "Remember when you were on that roof with the screaming raccoon and you forgot who you were, Miss Poulet?"

"Yes," said Francine.

"And then you remembered," said Frank.

"Yes," said Francine.

"It's good to know who you are," said Frank.

"I'm the genuine article, kid," said Francine. "And so are you. Now, let's concentrate. Let's keep our eyes open."

"My eyes are always open, Miss Poulet," said Frank.

"That's true," said Francine. "You're solid. You're certain. You hum, kid. You hum."

For Holly
K. D.

For Cricket and Dylan, who went west
C. V.

Tales from Deckawoo Drive

Volume Three

Where Are You Going, Baby Lincoln?

Chapter One

Baby Lincoln was dreaming.

In the dream, she was sitting on a train. Her hands were folded in her lap. The seat beside her was empty. Baby turned her head and looked out the window and saw that the dark sky was filled with stars, hundreds of them, thousands of them.

The train was going very fast, and the stars were falling through the sky, one after the other, chasing each other, leaving behind them great trails of light.

"Oh," said Baby, "shooting stars."

The train rushed through the starry darkness and Baby was entirely happy. *I wonder where I am headed,* she thought. *I cannot wait to find out. I am on a necessary journey.*

"Baby!" someone shouted. "You must wake up immediately!"

Baby woke up.

Her sister, Eugenia, was standing over her.

Eugenia had her hands on her hips.

"It is late, Baby. It is time to get on with our day," said Eugenia. "Goals must be set. Lists must be made. Tasks must be accomplished."

"Yes, Sister," said Baby.

At the breakfast table, Eugenia had Baby write down the day's goals.

Eugenia was very fond of goals.

"Goal number one," said Eugenia. She cleared her throat. "The mouse problem must be dealt with. We are on the verge of an infestation. You, Baby, will go to Clyde's Bait, Feed, Tackle, and Animal Necessities and purchase mousetraps."

"But mousetraps kill mice," said Baby.

"Exactly," said Eugenia.

"Oh, Sister," said Baby.

"Do not 'Oh, Sister' me. You are too soft for this world, Baby. You must be firm and resolute, particularly with mice. You must brook them no quarter."

Baby suddenly felt very tired.

She put her hands in her lap. She closed her eyes and saw the shooting stars from her dream. She remembered the words that had accompanied the stars. "Necessary journey," whispered Baby.

"Write it down," said Eugenia. "Write down *mousetraps*."

Baby sighed. She opened her eyes and picked up her pencil and wrote down the word *mouse*.

Eugenia looked over her shoulder. "You have not written the complete word," she said. "The complete word is *mousetraps.*"

From far away came the sound of a train whistle.

Eugenia tapped her finger on the table. "What are you waiting for, Baby? Write *traps.*"

The train whistle sounded again, closer this time.

"No," said Baby. She laid down the pencil.

"I beg your pardon?" said Eugenia.

"No," said Baby. "I will not write the word *traps.*" She pushed the paper away from her. She stood. She said, "Sister, I am going on a trip."

"Yes," said Eugenia. "You are. You are going to Clyde's Bait, Feed, Tackle, and Animal Necessities, and once you are there you will purchase mousetraps."

"No," said Baby. "I am going on a different kind of trip."

"A different kind of trip?" said Eugenia.

Baby closed her eyes, and again she saw the shooting stars. "I am going on a necessary journey."

"I don't know what you're talking about," said Eugenia.

Baby opened her eyes. She didn't know exactly what she was talking about either. But she knew that something important was happening. Her heart was beating very fast.

The sun was shining into the kitchen, and everything seemed outlined in brightness, possibility.

Eugenia stared at Baby. Her mouth was open. She looked quite astonished.

Baby was astonished, too.

She carefully pushed her chair under the table. She smoothed the front of her skirt. "Now," she said, "if you will excuse me, Sister, I must go and pack for my journey."

Chapter Two

Baby went into her bedroom and closed the door.

"What next?" she said out loud.

Well, the obvious thing was that she must pack a suitcase. That was what people did when they went on journeys.

Baby retrieved her suitcase from the top shelf of her closet and opened it. Several surprised and hopeful moths flew out of the emptiness.

Baby looked down at the open suitcase. She wasn't certain what to put in it.

She had no idea where she was going or how long she would be gone. Also, the last time she had packed a suitcase, Eugenia had been standing right next to her, telling her exactly what she must do and exactly how she must do it.

Baby thought for a while.

"A toothbrush," she said out loud. "I will definitely need a toothbrush."

She put her toothbrush in the suitcase. It looked lonely. She added a nightgown and reading glasses.

The reading glasses made Baby realize that she should bring along something to read.

She put her current library book into the suitcase. The book was a mystery entitled *The Inimitable Spigot*. Detective Henrik Spigot was a man with a mustache who was always telling other people what they should do and how they should do it. He was very judgmental. He was extremely certain.

Baby thought that Detective Spigot bore a strong resemblance to Eugenia. Except for the mustache, of course.

Baby was on page 23 of the book and so far she didn't think that Spigot was particularly inimitable.

She looked down at the book and her toothbrush and her nightgown. She added a sweater to the suitcase and then she closed the lid and snapped the buckles shut. The buckles were made of brass, and they made a lovely, definitive, necessary-journey kind of sound.

There was a knock at the door.

"Baby?" said Eugenia.

Baby opened the door. "Yes, Sister?" she said.

"I would like to ask you some questions about your journey," said Eugenia.

"All right," said Baby.

"Where are you going?" said Eugenia.

"I'm not certain," said Baby.

"*Why* are you going?" said Eugenia.

"I cannot say," said Baby.

"Stop this nonsense," said Eugenia.

"I will not stop," said Baby. She picked up her suitcase.

General Washington, who was Eugenia's cat, came slinking around the corner. He twined himself through Baby's legs so aggressively that she felt as if she might lose her balance.

"Moooowwwwwwwllllllll," said General Washington.

"General Washington is asking you not to go," said Eugenia in a somewhat subdued tone. "He is saying that he would like you to stay."

"What about you, Sister?" said Baby. "Would you like me to stay?" Baby knew, suddenly, that if Eugenia said the right words, she might put down her suitcase. She might stay.

Eugenia cleared her throat. She made a *harrump*-ish sort of noise. And then she straightened her shoulders.

"Far be it from me to tell you what to do," said Eugenia.

These were not the right words.

Baby tightened her grip on her suitcase. "If you will excuse me, Sister, I must leave now," said Baby. "It is necessary." She walked past Eugenia and General Washington.

Baby walked out the front door and down the front path and onto Deckawoo Drive. She took a right.

The suitcase was not heavy at all.

The sun was shining, and Baby's heart felt like a hummingbird in her chest. It was whirring. She could feel the flutter of its tiny wings.

She walked quickly. She did not look behind her. She was worried that Eugenia might be following her.

She was also a tiny bit hopeful that Eugenia might be following her.

When Baby was almost at the end of the block, she heard someone call her name.

"Baby! Baby Lincoln, wait for me!"

Baby stopped. She turned around.

Stella, who lived next door to the Lincolns, was running toward her.

"Where are you going, Baby Lincoln?"
said Stella.

Baby stood up straighter. She said,
"Hello, Stella. I am going on a necessary
journey."

Chapter Three

"Oh," said Stella, "I like journeys. I have taken lots of journeys, but I'm not sure I've ever been on a *necessary* journey. Most of my journeys have been family journeys, and that means we all go together in the car and my mother drives, and my father sleeps, and Frank navigates. When we are

on family journeys, we eat in restaurants,
and I always order a hot dog and Frank
doesn't order anything at all because he
brings a supply of peanut butter sandwiches
with him. He says that the peanut butter
sandwich is infallible. Do you like peanut
butter, Baby Lincoln?"

"I do like peanut butter," said Baby.

She felt a little niggle of worry. She realized that she had not packed anything to eat. She moved her suitcase from one hand to the other. She felt *The Inimitable Spigot* slide around in the near emptiness.

"The thing about our journeys," said Stella, "is that Frank is always the navigator. Always. I would like to hold the map sometimes. I would like to navigate. But I never get to."

"I understand," said Baby. "Eugenia will never allow me to hold the map either."

"Do you have a map?" said Stella. "We could look at it together."

"I do not have a map," said Baby. She felt another ping of worry.

"Well, where are you going?" said Stella.

"Right now?" said Baby.

218

"Right now," said Stella.

"I am headed to the train station," said Baby.

"I will walk with you," said Stella. She put her hand in Baby's hand. "Okay?"

"That would be lovely," said Baby.

At the train station, the ticket seller said, "Headed where?"

Stella said, "Her name is Baby Lincoln, and she is on a necessary journey."

"Uh-huh," said the ticket seller. "Headed where?"

"I'm not entirely certain," said Baby.

The ticket seller was holding a cheese sandwich in both hands. His name tag said LAWRENCE.

Lawrence looked at Baby. He looked at Stella. He sighed. He put the sandwich down on the counter. The cheese inside the sandwich was orange and there were several thick slices of it. It looked delicious. Baby wished that she had thought to make herself a cheese sandwich before leaving home.

Lawrence reached out and picked up a leaflet from the display in front of him.

"Schedule," he said, handing it to Baby. "Pick a destination."

"Thank you very much," said Baby.

"Let me see, let me see," said Stella.

They stepped away from the ticket counter and Baby handed Stella the schedule.

"Ohhhh," said Stella. "It's a chart. I'm really good with math and charts. Last year, Mrs. Wilkinson said that I was a true math whiz. Has anybody ever called you a true math whiz, Baby Lincoln?"

"Not that I can recall," said Baby.

Eugenia was the sister who had a head for figures. Or at least that was what Eugenia said.

Stella studied the schedule. "How much money do you have, Baby Lincoln? You can go to Calaband Darsh if you have enough money. Doesn't Calaband Darsh sound like a good place to go?"

Calaband Darsh sounded like a very grand place, a shooting-star kind of place. Baby opened her purse and took out her wallet. She handed the wallet to Stella and watched as Stella counted the money inside.

"Okay," said Stella. She handed the wallet back to Baby. She consulted the train schedule. "Let's see."

It turned out that Baby didn't have enough money to get to Calaband Darsh.

She had enough money to get to Fluxom.

"Fluxom?" said Baby.

"Fluxom," said Stella.

Fluxom did not sound like a shooting-star kind of place at all.

But Baby went bravely back to the ticket
counter and spoke to Lawrence. She said,
"One ticket for Fluxom, please."

And after that, there was no turning
back.

Baby boarded the train. Stella stood on the platform and waved good-bye.

The train lurched forward. Baby watched Stella get smaller and smaller until, finally, she disappeared altogether.

And then Baby Lincoln was alone, on a train, on a necessary journey.

Chapter Four

"Seat taken?" said a man wearing a gigantic fur hat.

The hat was so enormous and so furry that at first glance, Baby mistook the man for a bear.

"It is not taken," said Baby.

"Thank you very much," said the man. He sat down next to Baby. "Head allergies," he said. He pointed at his fur hat with an index finger. "I beg your pardon, but the hat must remain."

"Certainly," said Baby.

The man in the fur hat got out a news-paper. He skipped over the news and the sports and the opinions and went directly to the comics.

Eugenia said that the comics were a spectacular waste of time. Each morning, she removed them from the paper as a protest against their pointlessness.

The man in the fur hat followed each word of the comics with one enormous finger. He laughed softly as he read.

"Good for the head allergies," the man said to Baby when he saw her staring at him.

"I beg your pardon?" said Baby.

"Laughing," said the man. "Clears the sinuses and the soul in a very satisfying way."

"I see," said Baby. "Thank you."

The man rustled the pages of the paper. He laughed some more. And then he folded the paper carefully and took out a handkerchief and blew his nose for what seemed like a very long time.

He turned to Baby. "Did you bring something to read?"

"I brought my library book," said Baby. "It is a mystery entitled *The Inimitable Spigot.*"

"Is it funny?" said the man.

"It is not," said Baby. "My sister, Eugenia, recommended it to me."

"Would you care for a page of the comics?" said the man.

"Eugenia says that the comics are a spectacular waste of time."

The man in the fur hat laughed very loudly. "Why, of course they are." He slapped his knee. He laughed some more. "A spectacular waste of time! Absolutely! Yes. That is exactly what they are, bless them." He sneezed. He took out his handkerchief and blew his nose. He chuckled.

And then he turned to Baby with a very serious look on his face. "You must read the comics," he said. "I insist." The man unfolded the paper and handed Baby a page of the comics.

To be polite, Baby took the page. She held it out in front of her and placed a finger under each word in the first comic, just as she had seen the man in the fur hat do.

She glanced over at him.

"That's right," he said. "Keep going."

Baby looked at the pictures and read the words. In the first strip, there was a little man who had antennae on his head and who spoke in a strange language that resembled English just enough that Baby could make some sense of it. "Fozwhat mortak, I greet you!" said the man with the antennae. The picture showed him bending over, smiling at a bug on the sidewalk.

Baby read this and laughed. "Fozwhat mortak!" she said out loud.

"Yes!" said the man in the fur hat.

Baby went on to the next comic, which featured a squirrel that was able to fly and that was engaged in fighting evil. This strip was not quite as funny, but it was deeply satisfying in some ridiculous way. A squirrel! Fighting evil! Baby smiled to herself as she read it.

"You see?" said the man in the fur hat.

"I do!" said Baby.

Baby read the comics. She laughed. The man in the fur hat sat beside her, blowing his nose, nodding and smiling. Outside the train window, the world rushed by in a blur of green and gold and brown.

And Baby was suddenly tremendously
happy, just as she had been in her dream.

"Lower Loring!" shouted the conductor. "Lower Loring."

"This is my stop," said the man in the fur hat. He stood. He lifted the hat off his head and bowed to Baby. "It has been a pleasure, a delight, a revelation. It has been everything except a spectacular waste of time. Fozwhat mortak! I bid you safe travels. Tell your sister, Eugenia, that I send her greetings. Tell her to laugh."

Baby doubted that she would deliver this message to Eugenia, but she did think that she might start reading the comics on a regular basis.

"Good-bye," said Baby. "And thank you."

The man put the fur hat back on his head and lumbered down the aisle.

He really did look very much like a bear.

Baby heard him sneeze before he exited the train.

Chapter Five

Baby opened her suitcase and took out *The Inimitable Spigot.* She tried to read, but the book was not funny. Also, Henrik Spigot was annoying, and bossy. He thought he knew the answer to everything.

Baby closed the book and looked at the picture of Detective Spigot on the cover.

"No one knows the answer to everything," Baby said to Detective Spigot.

He really did look a lot like Eugenia—minus the mustache, of course.

Baby wondered what Eugenia was doing. Was she at Clyde's Bait, Feed, Tackle, and Animal Necessities? Was she purchasing mousetraps?

Did she miss Baby?

In answer to this last question, Baby heard Eugenia say, "Most certainly not!"

It was a very sad answer, even if it was an imaginary one.

Baby closed her eyes. She fell asleep.

When she woke up, a young woman was sitting beside her. The woman had long blond hair. There was a gigantic bag of jelly beans in her lap.

"Hi," said the woman. She smiled. "You were talking in your sleep. Something about mousetraps. I'm Sheila Marsden."

"I am Baby Lincoln," said Baby. "How do you do?"

"Baby?" said Sheila.

"Baby," said Baby.

"Your parents named you *Baby*?"

"No," said Baby. "That is what my sister, Eugenia, named me. Very early on, Eugenia said, 'I don't care what her name is. I am going to call her Baby. She is the baby, my baby.' And so I became Baby. And remained Baby."

"Wow," said Sheila. "That's kind of intense. What's your real name?"

"Lucille Abigail Eleanor Lincoln," said Baby. It felt strange to say her real name.

Sometimes Baby even forgot she had one.

"Lucille Abigail Eleanor Lincoln," repeated Sheila. "Cool. I like that name. Do you want a jelly bean, Lucille?"

Sheila held out the bag of jelly beans. Baby selected a yellow one. "Eugenia often says that jelly beans are bad for the teeth," said Baby. She put the jelly bean in her mouth. It tasted like sunshine. "Eugenia is not a fan of the jelly bean."

"That doesn't surprise me," said Sheila. "Have another one." She held out the bag again.

Baby selected a green jelly bean. It tasted like green leaves, things growing, springtime. She closed her eyes and chewed. The jelly bean was wonderful.

"So, where are you headed, Lucille?"

Lucille? Who was Lucille? And then Baby remembered. *She* was Lucille.

"I don't know where I'm headed," said Baby. "Well, I do know. I'm going to Fluxom. But it is more complicated than that. You see, I am on a necessary journey."

"That's cool," said Sheila. "Necessary journeys are cool. I'm on my way back to college, which is necessary, I guess." She shook the jelly bean bag. "Have another one," she said.

Baby selected a white jelly bean. She wondered if it would taste like snow.

"You can take more than one at a time, you know," said Sheila. "You can take a whole handful if you want to."

Baby leaned in closer to Sheila. She considered the bag. She took a purple jelly bean and a white one with yellow spots and several more green ones. She put them all in her mouth at once and chewed. Baby hadn't realized how hungry she was. She was glad that Sheila Marsden and her jelly bean bag had shown up.

Baby leaned back in her seat. The train seemed to be going faster, and from somewhere far away Baby heard music. It was a song that she knew but couldn't quite place.

"Do you hear music?" she said to Sheila.

"I hear something," said Sheila. She closed her eyes. She was quiet. "I've got a physics professor who says that the stars sing to each other all the time. Isn't that cool? Maybe the music we're hearing is the stars singing."

Did the stars really sing? Why had no one told Baby that before?

"Have another jelly bean, Lucille," said Sheila.

Baby leaned forward to inspect the jelly beans. Sunlight streamed in through the train window. Dust motes danced in the beams of light. Baby could still hear the music playing somewhere very far away. She felt another wave of happiness wash over her.

"Take a handful," said Sheila.

Baby took a handful.

Chapter Six

Sheila got off the train at Hickam Briar. She stood on the platform and waved to Baby. She called out, "Good-bye, Lucille! Good-bye!"

Sheila left Baby with an assortment of jelly beans tied up in a handkerchief. The handkerchief had Sheila's initials embroidered on it.

"See?" said Sheila when she gave Baby the handkerchief. "S.A.M. Those are my initials. Sheila Ann Marsden. My father embroidered that. He is very good with a needle and thread. If he knew you, he would sew your initials onto a handkerchief, too. Lucille Abigail Eleanor Lincoln. L.A.E.L."

Baby thought that she would miss Sheila quite a bit, but she didn't have time to miss her, because soon after the Hickam Briar station, the conductor appeared in the aisle by Baby's seat. With the conductor was a very small boy with a paper crown on his head and a sign around his neck. The sign said TRAVELING ALONE. PLEASE TREAT WITH EXTREME CARE, GENTLENESS, AND ALSO SOME CAUTION. HEADED TO FLATIRON IN CARE OF HIS AUNT GERTRUDE.

"My goodness," said Baby.

"I was wondering if you could keep an eye on this boy," said the conductor. "I was wondering if you could, uh, protect him."

The boy looked deeply unhappy. His eyes were red. His crown was crooked.

"Me?" said Baby.

No one had ever asked her to protect anyone.

"Yes," said the conductor. "You."

"Of course," said Baby. "I would be delighted."

"Good," said the conductor. "As the sign says, the boy is traveling alone."

The conductor cleared his throat. "And he is worried that, uh, wolves might attack the train."

"Wolves?" said Baby.

"That is his concern," said the conductor. "He has expressed it to me several times in a very, uh, vehement fashion. Wolves. Attacking the train."

The boy crossed his arms over his sign. He looked down at the floor. He was really very small to be traveling alone.

"You sit here," said the conductor to the boy, "in the aisle seat, see? And if the wolves come in through the window like you say they will, then they will, uh, get to this lady first, and that will slow them down some, right? Okay?"

"My goodness," said Baby. An image of the wolf from "Little Red Riding Hood" popped into her head. His teeth gleamed in a menacing way. Baby shook her head to dispel the wolf. She patted the seat beside her and smiled at the boy. "Sit down," she said.

The boy sat down and the conductor heaved a dramatic sigh. "Right," he said. "Good luck to both of you."

The conductor walked away, and the boy sat staring straight ahead with his arms still crossed over his sign.

"Well," said Baby. "Here we are."

"I'm not supposed to talk to strangers," said the boy.

"Of course," said Baby. "I understand." She got out Sheila's handkerchief and untied the knot. "Would you care for a jelly bean?" she said.

"I'm not supposed to take candy from strangers," said the boy.

"But I've been assigned to protect you," said Baby.

The boy looked up at Baby. His eyes were a bright blue. He looked down at the jelly beans.

It became very quiet on the train.

The boy sighed. He said, "Wolves have very sharp teeth."

Baby nodded.

"And when wolves get hungry, they do terrible things," said the boy. "Like attack trains."

Baby nodded again. "I believe you," she said. "Have a jelly bean."

The boy leaned forward. He unfolded his arms. He selected a yellow jelly bean.

"My name is George," he said.

Baby felt a small shiver of happiness.

"George is a wonderful name," said
Baby. "I am glad to meet you, George.
My name is Lucille."

And saying her name, her real name,
caused Baby to feel another ripple of joy.

Chapter Seven

George said, "I thought that this yellow jelly bean would taste like lemon, but it tastes like pear."

"Do you like it?" said Baby.

George nodded. "I like pears. My aunt Gertrude has lots and lots of pear trees in her backyard. She probably has a hundred pear trees. I am going to stay with my aunt Gertrude. But I only agreed to go because of the pears."

Baby nodded.

"Something terrible has happened," said George.

"Oh, dear," said Baby.

"Something horrible," said George.

"Does it have to do with wolves?" said Baby.

And then, to Baby's horror and dismay, George started to cry.

It was a crisis. And Eugenia was the sister who was good in a crisis, not Baby.

"Oh, no," said Baby. "Oh, dear." She emptied the jelly beans onto her lap and handed Sheila Marsden's monogrammed handkerchief to George. Her hands were shaking.

"I am so afraid," said George. He clutched the handkerchief. He cried louder.

Baby understood being afraid. When she was young, she had been afraid of everything: bats, bicycles, dusk, the darkness that followed dusk. Doorbells. She had, for some reason, been absolutely terrified of doorbells. Being alone had frightened her. And so had Mondays.

Eugenia was afraid of nothing, of course.

But whenever Baby had been afraid, Eugenia would sit with her in the green chair in the living room and read aloud to her. There was a lamp next to the green chair and the lamp made a yellow pool of light, and inside that pool of light, sitting next to Eugenia, Baby had been safe.

Baby felt a sudden, sharp pain high up in her chest.

She missed Eugenia.

George hiccupped. He used Sheila's handkerchief to blow his nose. "This handkerchief smells like jelly beans," he said. He took a deep breath and started to cry again.

"When I was a girl, I was frightened all the time," said Baby. "And when I was particularly frightened, my older sister would read to me, and that always made me feel safe. Would you like to hear a story?"

George nodded. "Yes," he said.

But then Baby remembered that the only book she had was *The Inimitable Spigot*. Her heart fell. She did not think that *The Inimitable Spigot* was the kind of book that would cheer anybody up. But she supposed it would have to do.

Baby opened the book. "Page One, Chapter One," said Baby.

George snuffled.

"'Detective Henrik Spigot was an extraordinary man, and was recognized by the department of police, the town of Winsome, and the whole of humanity as such. No mystery was truly a mystery to Detective Spigot—or at least it did not remain a mystery for long.

"'Detective Spigot lived alone in a green house on a high hill, and from there he could see the whole of Winsome spread out below him. The detective watched the people of the town from up high on his hill. He waited.'"

Baby paused.

George blew his nose into the handkerchief.

Detective Spigot is smug, Baby thought. *I do not care for him.*

George took a great gulp of air and held it in and then let it go in a *whoosh*.

"Aren't you going to read?" he said.

"Yes," said Baby. "But I was reading the wrong story."

"It wasn't much good," said George.

"I know," said Baby. "I will read the right story now."

"Good," said George.

Baby cleared her throat. She flipped to the middle of the book. She held *The Inimitable Spigot* up in front of her. "Chapter One," she said. "Once upon a time, there was a king. The king was wise and good. But he was lonely. And sometimes, late at night, he would stand in his garden and watch as stars fell through the night sky, chasing each other. The king was certain that he could hear music, the sound of the stars calling out to each other in the darkness. The music comforted the king."

Baby paused. The words she was reading weren't on the page at all. She, Lucille Abigail Eleanor Lincoln, was making them up.

"Keep going," said George.
And Baby did.

Chapter Eight

"The king had not always been a king. Once, he had been a boy who lived with his aunt in a small house on the side of a long, dark road. And behind this house, there grew pear trees, hundreds of them.

"The pear trees had been planted by a wizard named Calaband Darsh. And at the same time that the wizard planted the pear trees, he also cast a spell so that the boy, when he looked upon a pear, was able to see the entire universe hidden there. And this, it turned out, was a very good thing for a king to be able to do."

Baby felt George leaning in toward her.

She turned the page. "But I am getting ahead of myself. This is a long story," she read. Or pretended to read. "And it must be told right. All stories involving kings and wizards and wolves are important and must be told in a certain way and in their own time."

"There are wolves in this story?" said George.

"Of course," said Baby.

"Good," said George. "Keep going."

Baby read on.

The words of the story came to her without her thinking too much about what they should be. It was as if she were reading a book that already existed, telling a story that she already knew.

As she read, George leaned in closer and closer until, finally, he was leaning right up against her. He was warm. He smelled like peanut butter and construction paper.

"The wolves obeyed no man, of course," said Baby. "But they would sit and listen to the king. He could make it so that his human words made sense to their wolf ears and wolf hearts."

Baby looked down at George.

"Should I keep reading?" she said.

"Keep reading," said George.

It was late afternoon and the train was making a clickety-clackety sound as it headed through the universe.

Baby kept reading.

George's aunt Gertrude was waiting for him on the platform in Flatiron.

"That's her," said George. "There she is." He pointed.

Aunt Gertrude looked worried and flustered. She looked kind.

Baby's heart gave a small ping. Who would be waiting for her on the platform in Fluxom?

Eugenia would not be standing there. Eugenia was surely very, very angry at Baby for running away.

Eugenia was terrifying when she was angry. Baby's heart gave another, different kind of ping.

"Good-bye," said George.

He stood. He adjusted his crown. "Thank you for reading me the story. I could tell that you were making it up."

"You could?" said Baby.

George nodded. "I'm small," he said. "But I can read."

"Oh," said Baby. She was strangely disappointed.

"I need to know what happened to the king," said George.

"Well," said Baby. She felt a flush of happiness, certainty. "I will write to you. I will tell you what happens next."

"All of it?" said George. "The whole story?"

"Every bit of it," said Baby.

The conductor came to escort George off the train. Baby lowered the window. She shouted out to Aunt Gertrude. She said, "Hello, I am a friend of George and my name is Lucille Lincoln. I live at

274

Fifty-two Deckawoo Drive in Gizzford. If you write to me, I will write to George."

Aunt Gertrude smiled. She waved. She said, "Lucille at Fifty-two Deckawoo Drive! We will write to you!"

And then George was on the platform. Aunt Gertrude hugged him. She enveloped him.

The train started to move.

Aunt Gertrude and George waved at Baby, and Baby waved back.

"Good-bye, Lucille," shouted George.

His golden paper crown glinted in the last of the evening light.

Baby leaned back in her seat and closed her eyes. She thought about the house on Deckawoo Drive and the way the sun shone on the kitchen table in the early morning and again, from a different angle, in the late afternoon.

She thought about Eugenia sitting at the table.

Baby's heart clenched.

She wanted to go home.

Chapter Nine

It was dark in Fluxom.

The station platform was empty.

"Fluxom!" shouted the conductor. "Disembark for Fluxom!"

Baby took hold of her suitcase. She stood. The conductor helped her down the metal stairs.

And then the train pulled away and Baby was alone on the platform.

Somewhere, hidden in some scraggly bush by the train tracks, a cricket sang. The song was high and sweet and it made Baby feel even more lonely. She thought about the stars and how they sang to each other. She listened very closely, but she could not hear their music. She could only hear the lone cricket.

"Baby!" someone shouted.

Baby saw Eugenia and Stella walking toward her. Her heart thumped once, twice, three times. First it thumped in disbelief (Eugenia had come) and then it thumped in gratitude (Eugenia had come for her) and then, finally, it thumped with joy (Eugenia had come for Baby!).

"Baby Lincoln!" called Stella. "We came to meet your train! I knew where you were going and what time you would arrive because I was the one who read the train schedule. And I thought it would be very bad if you got off the train and no one was here to meet you. Wouldn't that have been very bad? And so Mr. Watson and Eugenia Lincoln and Mercy Watson and me drove all the way here. I navigated! I held the map! And Eugenia Lincoln was upset because she did not get to hold the map. And she was also upset because Mercy got to sit in the front seat. Mr. Watson and Mercy are waiting in the car, and you can hold the map on the way home if you want to, Baby Lincoln."

"This is all just ridiculous," said Eugenia. "It is absurd! I can't believe we drove with a pig in the front seat to the middle of nowhere."

"Oh, Sister," said Baby. "I missed you so."

Eugenia sniffed. She looked away.

"Eugenia missed you back!" said Stella. She jumped up and down. "She missed you and missed you and missed you. It's true. It's all she could talk about. 'Where is Baby? We must find Baby? What will I ever do without Baby? I would be lost without Baby.' That is what Eugenia said."

"Is that true, Sister?" said Baby. "Would you be lost without me?"

"Perhaps," said Eugenia. She stared off at the horizon.

"Tell her," said Stella. She took hold of Eugenia's hand and swung it back and forth.

"I missed you," whispered Eugenia. "I would be lost without you, Baby."

"Oh, Sister," said Baby.

"See?" said Stella. "*See?* You are two sisters who love each other. But we have to go now because Mr. Watson and Mercy are in the car and Mercy is hungry and the engine is running and it is a long drive. We have to go home. Let's go home."

"Let's," said Baby.

"Let's," said Eugenia. She picked up Baby's suitcase.

"Oh, Sister," said Baby. "I have so much to tell you."

Eugenia took hold of Baby's right hand. She said, "Well, if you insist on telling a story, I suppose I will have to listen."

Stella took hold of Baby's left hand. "We can talk and talk and talk," said Stella. "And when we get home, it will be almost morning and maybe Mrs. Watson will make us some toast with a great deal of butter on it."

Coda

An envelope arrived at 52 Deckawoo Drive.

The envelope was addressed to Lucille Lincoln, and there were two letters inside.

The first letter said:

Dear Lucille,

I am writing to you on behalf of my nephew George whom you met on a train journey. George sends you greetings and has enclosed a letter of his own. He is well and happy. Although he does sometimes worry about wolves. Thank you for your kindness.

Yours truly,

Gertrude Nissbaum

The second letter said:

Dear Lucille,
Will you tell me the rest of the story?

Love, George

▶ ▶ ▶

Every morning began the same way:
Baby sat at the kitchen table and read
the comics, all of them. She laughed.
She blew her nose.

When she was done with the comics,
Baby got out a notebook and a pencil
and worked at writing down the story
of the good king named George and
the great wizard called Calaband Darsh.
She told a story of wolves and pear trees
and singing stars, a story of good and
evil and hope.

Eugenia sat across the table from
Baby and wrote her list of goals.

The morning light came streaming
into the kitchen.

Baby wrote her story.

She ate jelly beans as she worked.

Francine Poulet Meets the Ghost Raccoon: Tales from Deckawoo Drive, Volume Two
Library of Congress Catalog Card Number 2014951801
ISBN 978-0-7636-6886-0 (hardcover)
ISBN 978-0-7636-9088-5 (paperback)

Where Are You Going, Baby Lincoln? Tales from Deckawoo Drive, Volume Three
Library of Congress Catalog Card Number 2016940244
ISBN 978-0-7636-7311-6 (hardcover)
ISBN 978-0-7636-9758-7 (paperback)

ISBN 978-1-5362-0864-1 (paperback collection)

20 21 22 23 24 TRC 11 10 9 8 7 6

Printed in Eagan, MN, U.S.A.

This book was typeset in Mrs. Eaves.
The illustrations were done in gouache.

Candlewick Press
99 Dover Street
Somerville, Massachusetts 02144

visit us at www.candlewick.com

Every porcine wonder was once a piglet!

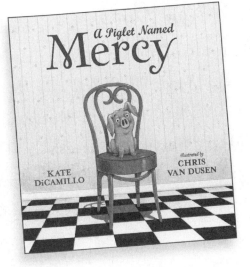

In this picture book, a tiny piglet brings love (and chaos) to Deckawoo Drive.

www.candlewick.com

Kate DiCamillo is the beloved author of many books for young readers, including the Mercy Watson and Deckawoo Drive series. Her books *Flora & Ulysses* and *The Tale of Despereaux* both received Newbery Medals. A former National Ambassador for Young People's Literature, Kate DiCamillo lives in Minneapolis.

Chris Van Dusen is the author-illustrator of *The Circus Ship, King Hugo's Huge Ego, Randy Riley's Really Big Hit,* and *Hattie & Hudson,* and the illustrator of the Mercy Watson and Deckawoo Drive series as well as Mac Barnett's *President Taft Is Stuck in the Bath.* He lives in Maine.

Kate DiCamillo is the beloved author of many books for young readers, including the Mercy Watson and Deckawoo Drive series. Her books *Flora & Ulysses* and *The Tale of Despereaux* both received Newbery Medals. A former National Ambassador for Young People's Literature, Kate DiCamillo lives in Minneapolis.

Chris Van Dusen is the author-illustrator of *The Circus Ship, King Hugo's Huge Ego, Randy Riley's Really Big Hit,* and *Hattie & Hudson,* and the illustrator of the Mercy Watson and Deckawoo Drive series as well as Mac Barnett's *President Taft Is Stuck in the Bath.* He lives in Maine.

Every porcine wonder was once a piglet!

In this picture book, a tiny piglet brings love (and chaos) to Deckawoo Drive.